MW00909581

Captain Blownaparte and the Golden Skeleton
Part One

by Helga Hopkins
Illustrated by David Benham

First published as an eBook in 2014
Paperback edition published in 2018

contact@blownaparte.com

ISBN-13: 978-1720777304
ISBN-10: 1720777306

Captain Blownaparte™
and the Golden Skeleton

by Helga Hopkins & David Benham

Part One: The Golden Neck Bones

Part 1 The Golden Neck Bones

Captain Blownaparte and his crew were celebrating on their famous pirate ship, 'The Battered Cod'. They'd just won their first victory against the dastardly pirate, Captain Purplebeard, and the deck was piled high with large treasure chests packed full of gold coins. But Sproggie, Captain Blownaparte's nephew, was only interested in one small treasure chest: the one they'd found secretly hidden in Captain Purplebeard's cabin! 'Go on then boy - open the chest,' chuckled the Captain. Sproggie gingerly opened the lid and let out a disappointed sigh, 'Awww! - Just another load of boring old gold coins.'

'But I LOVE gold coins,' boomed the Captain, sticking his hand deep into the chest and wiggling his fingers about in glee. Then suddenly he pulled it out with a painful yelp! There, clamped firmly to his hand, was a glistening golden skull. But, seeing Captain Blownaparte, the skull quickly let go and tumbled back into the chest. Everyone stared open mouthed. 'Who on earth are you?' asked Sproggie fearfully. The Golden Skull impatiently clattered his jaw from side to side, explaining that he'd once been the Captain of a large and beautiful ship, but had fallen foul of a nasty ghost captain, who'd turned him into a golden skeleton. His only chance of turning back into a human again was finding someone to help him track down the rest of his golden bones.

Now, little Sproggie had a very soft heart, and immediately volunteered that they should all help the skeleton. The rest of the crew fancied a decent adventure and all chimed in with their agreement. The Skull told them that his neck bones were hooked on a chain round Captain Gingerbeard's neck. This notorious pirate was one of Captain Purplebeard's many nasty brothers. 'You'll be lucky getting to him,' chirped Rosie, 'He lives in a castle on a high cliff from where he spies on treasure ships so he can rob them. The castle is so well guarded we'll never get in.' So Prosper, the ships clever parrot, scratched his beak thoughtfully and came up with the perfect answer. They'll deliver themselves to the castle – but secretly hidden in a wine barrel!

Later, Captain Blownaparte, Sproggie, and Turnip, the ship's pet rat, all squeezed themselves very tightly into a wine barrel. Sproggie took along a rucksack full of sticky toffee too. This was the Captain's legendary secret weapon. Pedro, the strongest member of the crew, carried the barrel up to the castle, where a grumpy guard took it off him and rolled it down into the cellar with a big kick! Prosper, however, had secretly flown into the cellar through an open skylight, and tapped on the barrel when the coast was clear.

Panting and spluttering, Captain Blownaparte and Sproggie crawled out. Turnip however, was enjoying the fun, especially when a couple of his rat cousins peeped out to see what was going on. Luckily they were only too pleased to show Turnip a hidden staircase which joined up to the castle's secret passage. The Captain set off first, and the others rather fearfully followed behind.

The crooked staircase was deathly dark and led upstairs to a narrow winding passage. Sproggie didn't like it one little bit. It was full of dust and cobwebs and, worst of all, giant spiders! Suddenly Sproggie was stopped in his tracks by a most delicious smell. In fact it was so delicious he quite forgot himself - until suddenly his eyes met the biggest spider he'd ever seen in his life! Sproggie desperately tried to wriggle away when disaster struck. Right underneath him a crack opened up in the floor and the poor boy tumbled through it - right onto the table in the castle kitchen, where an enormous pot was being stirred. 'Heavens!' screamed the cook. 'There's a boy in my soup!'

'Quickly! - we've got to divert attention away from Sproggie so the Captain can hook him out of the soup,' whispered Prosper in Turnip's ear. So Prosper fluttered into the kitchen and perched on a steaming plum pudding. 'Oh No!' screamed another cook! – 'There's a parrot on my pudding!' Turnip didn't want to be left out and scuttled after Prosper into the kitchen and plunged head first into an enormous bowl of custard. 'Oh no!' screamed yet another cook, 'There's a rat in my custard!'

While all eyes were on Turnip and Prosper, Captain Blownaparte hooked Sproggie out of the soup and bundled him back along the secret passage. Quick as a flash they were joined by Prosper, who was munching a large helping of plum pudding, and a truly bedraggled Turnip, who was dripping all over in bright yellow custard! After going round in circles they finally reached the top room of the castle, which was blocked by a big wooden door. Through the keyhole they saw Captain Gingerbeard behind his telescope, spying on passing treasure ships.

Suddenly Sproggie had a brilliant idea and whispered it to Captain Blownaparte, 'You keep Gingerbeard busy, and I'll see to the rest,' said the little boy. Slowly and silently they opened the door and crept into the room. But when Gingerbeard turned and saw them, he quickly drew his sword! 'Blasted Captain Blownaparte! I'll finish you once and for all!' boomed the nasty pirate. But Sproggie had sneaked behind Gingerbeard and smeared a load of sticky toffee around the brass eyepiece of the telescope.

Then, in the confusion, Prosper shouted, 'HUGE treasure ship coming up over there!' On hearing this, Gingerbeard abandoned Captain Blownaparte and dashed over to the telescope and pressed his eye hard on the eyepiece. 'WHAT treasure ship?!' he thundered. But when he tried to move his eye away, he found he was well and truly glued on by the sticky toffee! 'I think I'll look after this in future,' giggled Captain Blownaparte as he smartly removed the golden bones from around Gingerbeard's neck.

'You'll never get out of here alive!' screamed Gingerbeard. But Captain Blownaparte simply grinned as he and the others ran up a spiral staircase leading to the outside terrace on the very top of the castle. Suddenly, they found themselves among several large cannons pointing towards passing ships, and a large bed sheet fluttering on a washing line. 'Oh dear,' said Captain Blownaparte, 'I took the wrong door. I think we're well and truly trapped.' 'No we're not,' Prosper said with a steely look in his eyes. 'If you follow my instructions we'll simply fly away from the castle.'

He told the Captain and Sproggie to turn a nearby table upside down and glue the four corners of the bed sheet to the four table legs with some sticky toffee. Next, they glued a piece of rope round a cannon ball and loaded it into the cannon while the other end of the rope was tied to the table. Turnip shook his head at Sproggie. 'I think Prosper has gone a little bit bonkers!' Prosper then told them all to perch on the upturned table. Then he lit the cannon and fluttered in with them. Seconds later the cannon ball shot out with an enormous big bang, yanking the upturned table along behind it!

In a flash they were flying over the sea! 'This is so brilliant!' laughed Sproggie. 'Ohhhh Yesssss! And don't forget to fasten your seat belts,' yelled the Captain. Although Turnip had gone a little bit green, Prosper couldn't resist teasing him with a few choice words. 'So who's the mad one now Turnip?' Before long they saw their ship below them, and Prosper yelled at the Captain to use his cutlass leg to slice through the rope holding the table onto the cannon ball. Then, magically, the bed sheet billowed out like a parachute and they slowly glided down to the ship. The crew were happy to see them back alive, and the Golden Skull was delighted at getting his neck bones back.

'So, what's next?' asked Sproggie eagerly. Captain Blownaparte groaned. 'Well,' said the Skull, 'I think I know where my right arm is hidden, but it's not going to be easy. It's in a dark cave belonging to a very large, and extremely bad tempered sea serpent.' 'Ohhhh No! - I absolutely hate snakes and serpents,' puffed Alfredo. 'OK then, let's have a big feast first,' said Captain Blownaparte, 'It's never a good idea to start a new adventure on an empty stomach.' Everybody cheered, and before long the delicious aroma of the crew's favourite fish pie was wafting up their noses!

The End

PEDRO   ROSIE   CAPTAIN
BLOWNAPARTE   SPROGGIE

PROSPER

SPIKE

PIRATE TIDY   ALFREDO   SWISS SEPP

TURNIP

Made in the USA
Monee, IL
06 May 2021